AF407775

WHERE LOVE LIVES FOREVER

Aiden Blake

Copyright © 2024 by DAIAN Books.

All rights reserved. No part of this book may be used or reproduced in any form whatsoever without written permission except in the case of brief quotations in critical articles or reviews.

This book is a work of fiction. Names, characters, businesses, organizations, places, events and incidents either are the product of the author's imagination or are used fictitiously. Any resemblance to actual persons, living or dead, events, or locales is entirely coincidental.

Printed in the United States of America.

For more information, or to book an event, contact :
urbanheroesl@outlook.com
https://bit.ly/3yBHV5j

Cover design by DAIAN Books

ISBN - Paperback : 979-8-3302-2531-6

First Edition : June 2024

CONTENTS

To the LGBTQ+ Community,

This is for every soul who has ever felt different, who has ever loved against the odds, who has ever faced the world with courage in their hearts. Whether you stand alone or hand in hand with another, know this: there is someone for everyone.

You are seen, you are valued, and you are loved. In a world that can often be unkind, your authenticity shines as a beacon of hope and strength. Each of you is a testament to the beauty of diversity, the power of love, and the unbreakable spirit of the human heart.

To those in loving relationships, may your bond be a source of endless joy and support. To those still searching, believe that the universe has a special someone for you. Your story is not just one of perseverance, but one of inevitable connection and boundless love.

Remember, you are never alone. Your

community stands beside you, celebrating every triumph and supporting you through every challenge. Embrace your journey, cherish your love, and never forget that you are worthy of all the happiness this world has to offer.

With all my heart,

Aiden

INTRODUCTION

Where Love Lives Forever

Love is a force that transcends the physical realm, defying the boundaries of life and death. In the heart-wrenching tale of Adam and Dennis, we are drawn into a world where love's ethereal power is both a source of boundless joy and a crucible of unimaginable pain. This story, steeped in the profound depths of human emotion, explores the tender journey of a love that endures beyond the grave and the courageous path to finding love once again.

Adam and Dennis's love story begins like a symphony, each note building towards a crescendo of happiness. Dennis, a concert pianist with striking blue eyes and golden hair, embodies charm and grace. His smile, radiant and genuine, lights up Adam's world, igniting a passionate romance that seems destined for eternity. Their bond is more than just physical attraction; it is a connection of souls, intertwined in a dance of love and understanding.

Their first year together is a mosaic of shared dreams and intimate moments. From romantic dinners under the stars to quiet evenings spent in each other's arms, Adam and Dennis build a life filled with love's purest expressions. Dennis's music becomes the soundtrack of their love, each melody a testament to their unbreakable bond. They share laughter, secrets, and a future that seems bright and limitless.

But life's cruel hand strikes without warning. A tragic car accident snatches Dennis away in an instant, leaving Adam shattered and alone. The world, once vibrant with love's colors, turns bleak and desolate. Adam's grief is a storm, relentless and consuming, driving him to the brink of despair. His heart, now a vessel of pain, longs for release, for an end to the unbearable torment of living without Dennis.

In his darkest moment, as Adam stands on the precipice of life and death, he feels a presence. A gentle touch on his shoulder, as familiar as it is unexpected, halts his fatal act. It is Dennis, not in the flesh, but in spirit. The love they shared transcends death, binding Dennis to the world he left too soon. Determined to save Adam from his grief, Dennis's spirit lingers, watching over his beloved, guiding him through the storm of sorrow.

The years that follow are a testament to the enduring power of love. Dennis's spirit becomes Adam's silent guardian, a comforting presence in moments of pain and a gentle nudge towards healing. Though unseen, Dennis's love is a constant, helping Adam navigate the turbulent waters of loss and heartache. Every whispered word, every tender touch, speaks of a love that death cannot diminish.

As time weaves its tapestry of healing, Adam begins to find strength. Slowly, the pieces of his shattered heart start to mend. He learns to smile again, to find joy in the world around him. And then, unexpectedly, love enters his life once more. A new man, kind and understanding, captures Adam's heart. This new love is different, yet deeply profound, offering Adam a chance at happiness once more.

Dennis, watching from beyond, feels a mixture of joy and sorrow. He wants Adam to move forward, to embrace this new love fully, yet hopes to never be forgotten. His spirit, bound by love and longing, struggles with the desire to let go and the need to remain a part of Adam's life.

"Where Love Lives Forever" is a story of love's resilience and the courage to let go. It is a journey through the depths of grief to the heights of new beginnings, a poignant reminder that love, in all its forms, is the most powerful force in the universe. This tale, filled with raw emotion and tender moments, will touch the hearts of readers, offering a beacon of hope and a testament to the enduring power of love.

1

THE BEGINNING OF FOREVER

Adam's life changed the moment he saw Dennis for the first time. It was at a charity gala, the kind of event Adam usually avoided. But that night, something pulled him there, a twist of fate that led him to the man who would become the center of his world.

Dennis was at the piano, his fingers dancing effortlessly over the keys. The music he played was mesmerizing, a beautiful blend of classical and contemporary that captivated everyone in the room. Adam couldn't take his eyes off him. Dennis's blue eyes sparkled with passion, his smile radiating warmth and joy. His blonde hair fell perfectly around his face, giving him an almost ethereal appearance.

When Dennis finished playing, the room erupted in applause. Adam, usually shy and reserved, found himself moving towards the piano, drawn by an invisible force. Dennis looked up, their eyes meeting across the room. In that instant, something clicked. It was as if their souls recognized each other, a spark of connection that neither could deny.

"Hi, I'm Adam," he said, his voice trembling slightly with nervous excitement.

Dennis smiled, a smile that lit up his entire face. "I'm Dennis. It's nice to meet you, Adam."

From that moment on, their lives were

intertwined. They spent hours talking, discovering shared interests and dreams. Dennis was not just a talented pianist; he was kind, funny, and deeply compassionate. He had a way of making Adam feel seen and understood, something Adam had longed for his entire life.

Their first date was magical. Dennis took Adam to a small, intimate jazz club. The music, the ambiance, and the company were perfect. They talked and laughed, losing track of time as they shared stories and experiences. Adam found himself opening up in ways he never had before, feeling safe and cherished in Dennis's presence.

As their relationship blossomed, they created a world of their own, filled with love, music, and laughter. They spent weekends exploring the city, discovering hidden gems and creating memories. Dennis would often play the piano for Adam, composing pieces that spoke of their love and connection. Each note was a declaration of his feelings, a promise of forever.

Their love was not without challenges. Both had past wounds that occasionally resurfaced, but together they faced them, growing stronger with each passing day. Dennis's music career was demanding, requiring frequent travel and long hours of practice. Adam, a writer, often struggled with his own insecurities and fears. But their love was a refuge, a sanctuary where they found strength and solace.

One evening, as they lay in bed, Dennis turned to Adam, his eyes filled with love and determination. "I love you, Adam. More than words can ever express. You are my everything, and I want to spend the rest of my life with you."

Tears filled Adam's eyes as he held Dennis close. "I love you too, Dennis. With all my heart. You've given me a love I never thought I'd find. Forever, I promise."

Their promise of forever seemed unbreakable, a bond that nothing could sever. They talked about their future, dreaming of a life filled with love and happiness. Dennis's career was soaring, and Adam's writing was gaining recognition. They were on top of the world, their love a beacon of hope and joy.

But fate, with its cruel and unpredictable nature, had other plans. The love that seemed destined for eternity was about to face a test that neither could have foreseen. A single moment, a tragic accident, would shatter their dreams and plunge Adam into a darkness he never imagined.

2

WHISPERS IN THE WIND

The day Dennis died started like any other. The sun was shining, the air was filled with the promise of a beautiful day, and Adam was writing at his desk, a smile playing on his lips as he thought about Dennis's latest performance. They had plans to celebrate that evening, a special dinner at their favorite restaurant to mark their one-year anniversary.

Dennis had left early for a rehearsal, his usual

cheerful self, blowing a kiss to Adam as he walked out the door. "See you tonight, love," he said, his voice filled with anticipation.

Adam watched him leave, his heart full of love and gratitude. He spent the day working on his latest manuscript, the hours slipping by unnoticed. As the afternoon turned to evening, he started getting ready for their date, excitement bubbling within him.

The phone call came just as he was about to leave. The voice on the other end was calm and professional, delivering the news with a detached precision that felt surreal. Dennis had been in a car accident, they said. He was gone, just like that.

The world around Adam crumbled. His legs gave way, and he collapsed to the floor, the phone slipping from his hand. A scream tore from his throat, a raw, primal sound of utter devastation. Dennis, his love, his life, was gone. The vibrant, joyful man who had brought so much light into his life was no more.

The days that followed were a blur. Friends and family tried to offer comfort, but their words were hollow, unable to pierce the fog of grief that enveloped Adam. He moved through the motions of living, but inside he felt dead, his heart shattered into a million pieces.

Everywhere he looked, he saw reminders of Dennis. The piano, now silent and covered in dust, the photographs of their happy moments, the scent of Dennis's cologne lingering in the air. Each memory was a dagger to his heart, a painful reminder of what he had lost.

Nights were the worst. Alone in their bed, Adam would lie awake, his mind replaying the last moments he had seen Dennis. He would cry until there were no tears left, his sobs echoing in the empty room. The pain was unbearable, a constant, gnawing ache that made him long for oblivion.

It was on one of those nights, when the darkness seemed too overwhelming, that Adam made the decision. He couldn't go on living without Dennis. The pain was too much, the emptiness too vast. He wanted to be with Dennis, wherever he was, to escape the torment of his grief.

With trembling hands, he wrote a note, a final goodbye to the world. Then, taking a razor blade, he prepared to end his suffering. As he brought the blade to his wrist, a strange sensation stopped him. It was as if a hand, warm and familiar, rested on his shoulder.

He froze, his breath catching in his throat. The room was silent, but he felt a presence, a comforting, loving presence that he knew instinctively. "Dennis?" he whispered, his voice breaking.

Tears streamed down his face as he dropped the blade, his heart pounding with a mixture of hope and sorrow. He closed his eyes, reaching out with his senses, desperate to feel Dennis's presence again. The touch on his shoulder remained, a gentle reminder that he was not alone.

In that moment, Adam knew that Dennis was still with him, in some inexplicable way. The love they had shared was too strong to be extinguished by death. Dennis's spirit, his essence, was still bound to Adam, guiding him away from the brink of despair.

The realization was both comforting and heartbreaking. Adam felt a glimmer of hope, a faint light in the darkness. Dennis had saved him, had given him a reason to hold on. But the pain of his loss was still overwhelming, a burden that he wasn't sure he could bear.

3

A YEAR OF BLISS

Before the tragedy that tore their world apart, Adam and Dennis had shared a year of pure bliss. Their relationship had been a whirlwind of joy and passion, a love story that seemed almost too perfect to be real.

Their first date had set the tone for their relationship. Dennis had a knack for making every moment special, infusing their time together with his unique blend of charm and spontaneity. They quickly became inseparable, spending as much time together as their busy lives allowed.

Weekends were their sanctuary. They would escape to the countryside, finding solace in nature's embrace. Dennis loved to play the piano under the open sky, his music blending with the sounds of the wind and birds. Adam would sit beside him, content to listen, feeling the music resonate deep within his soul.

Their love was a source of inspiration for Adam's writing. He found himself pouring his feelings into his stories, crafting tales of love and devotion that mirrored his own experiences. Dennis was his muse, his presence infusing Adam's words with a depth and emotion that captivated readers.

Dennis, too, found his creativity flourishing. He composed new pieces, each one a testament to his love for Adam. His concerts were a reflection of their relationship, each performance a passionate declaration of his feelings. The audiences were moved by the raw emotion in his music, sensing the love that fueled his artistry.

Their home was a haven of love and laughter. They decorated it together, each room a blend of their tastes and personalities. The living room was dominated by Dennis's grand piano, a beautiful instrument that had been a gift from Adam. They spent countless hours there, Dennis playing while Adam wrote, their creative energies harmonizing in perfect synchronicity.

Dinner time was a cherished ritual. They loved to cook together, experimenting with new recipes and sharing their favorite dishes. The kitchen was often filled with the sounds of laughter and playful banter, their connection growing stronger with each shared meal.

Their evenings were filled with simple pleasures. They would cuddle on the couch, watching movies or talking about their dreams and plans for the future. Dennis's touch was always reassuring, his presence a constant source of comfort and happiness for Adam.

As their one-year anniversary approached, Dennis planned a special surprise. He knew how much Adam loved surprises, and he wanted to make this milestone unforgettable. He booked a private concert hall and arranged for a candlelit dinner on the stage, surrounded by flowers and twinkling lights.

That night, Dennis played a piece he had composed specifically for Adam. The music was a reflection of their journey together, filled with moments of joy, passion, and tenderness. As the final notes faded, Dennis took Adam's hand, looking into his eyes with a love that took Adam's breath away.

"Adam, you are the love of my life," Dennis said, his voice trembling with emotion. "This past year has been the happiest of my life, and I can't imagine a future without you. Will you marry me?"

Tears filled Adam's eyes as he nodded, unable to speak. He threw his arms around Dennis, holding him tight as they both cried tears of joy. It was a moment of pure happiness, a promise of a future filled with love and shared dreams.

They spent the rest of the night talking about their plans, dreaming of a wedding that would be a celebration of their love. Dennis's music and Adam's words would blend together, creating a ceremony that was uniquely theirs. They were filled with excitement and anticipation, eager to embark on this new chapter of their lives.

But fate had other plans. The tragic accident that took Dennis away shattered their dreams, leaving Adam to navigate a world that had lost its light. Yet, even in the depths of his grief, the memory of their love remained a beacon of hope, guiding him through the darkness.

4

THE SHATTERING SILENCE

The silence that followed Dennis's death was deafening. The once vibrant home they had shared was now filled with an oppressive stillness, a constant reminder of the absence of the man who had brought so much life and joy into it.

Adam struggled to cope with the loss. The grief was a physical weight, pressing down on him, making it hard to breathe, to think, to exist. Each day was a battle, a struggle to find the strength to keep going. The routines that had once been comforting now felt empty and meaningless.

Friends and family tried to reach out, offering their support, but Adam found it hard to accept their help. He felt isolated, trapped in his own world of pain and sorrow. The well-meaning words of comfort often felt hollow, unable to penetrate the wall of grief that surrounded him.

Dennis's funeral was a blur of tears and condolences. Adam barely remembered the faces of those who came to pay their respects, their expressions of sympathy blending into a haze of sorrow. He stood by Dennis's casket, numb and disbelieving, struggling to accept the reality that his beloved was truly gone.

In the weeks that followed, Adam withdrew from the world. He stopped writing, unable to find the words that had once flowed so easily. The stories that had been his refuge now seemed distant and unattainable, the characters and plots a painful reminder of a life that no longer existed.

Nights were the worst. Alone in their bed, Adam would lie awake, his mind replaying the last moments he had seen Dennis. He would cry until there were no tears left, his sobs echoing in the empty room. The pain was unbearable, a constant, gnawing ache that made him long for oblivion.

One night, driven to the brink of despair, Adam decided he couldn't go on. The pain was too much, the emptiness too vast. He wanted to be with Dennis, to escape the torment of his grief. He wrote a note, a final goodbye to the world, and prepared to end his suffering.

But just as he was about to take the final step, he felt a presence. A gentle touch on his shoulder, as familiar as it was unexpected. It was as if Dennis was there, stopping him, guiding him away from the brink. The realization that Dennis's spirit was still with him, watching over him, gave Adam a reason to hold on.

In the days that followed, Adam began to sense

Dennis's presence more clearly. It was in the little things – the way a breeze would stir the curtains, the faint sound of music in the distance, the feeling of a hand on his shoulder when he was at his lowest. Dennis was there, a silent guardian, helping him navigate the turbulent waters of grief.

The knowledge that Dennis was still with him, in some inexplicable way, was both a comfort and a torment. Adam felt a glimmer of hope, a faint light in the darkness. But the pain of his loss was still overwhelming, a burden that he wasn't sure he could bear.

5

THE DARKNESS WITHIN

Adam's struggle with grief was far from over. Despite the comforting presence of Dennis's spirit, the darkness within him was a relentless force. Each day was a battle against the overwhelming sorrow that threatened to consume him.

He avoided the places they used to go together, the coffee shop where they had their first date, the park where they would walk hand in hand, the concert hall where Dennis's music had come to life. Every familiar place was a painful reminder of what he had lost, a trigger for the memories that both comforted and tormented him.

Adam's work suffered as well. Writing, once his greatest passion, had become an impossible task. The words that had flowed so easily now seemed distant and unattainable. His characters and plots were a painful reminder of a life that no longer existed. He felt disconnected from his own stories, unable to find solace in the fictional worlds he had created.

Friends and family continued to reach out, their concern evident in their eyes and voices. But Adam found it hard to accept their help. He felt isolated, trapped in his own world of pain and sorrow. The well-meaning words of comfort often felt hollow, unable to penetrate the wall of grief that surrounded him.

He spent hours at the piano, his fingers tracing the keys but never pressing them down. The silence was deafening, a constant reminder of Dennis's absence. He longed to hear Dennis's music again, to feel the joy and passion that had filled their home. But the piano remained silent, a symbol of his loss.

Nights were the hardest. Alone in their bed, Adam would lie awake, his mind replaying the last moments he had seen Dennis. He would cry until there were no tears left, his sobs echoing in the empty room. The pain was unbearable, a constant, gnawing ache that made him long for oblivion.

In his darkest moments, Adam would talk to Dennis, whispering his thoughts and feelings into the empty room. He found a strange comfort in these one-sided conversations, imagining Dennis's responses, feeling his presence even if he couldn't see him. It was a way to keep Dennis close, to hold on to the love they had shared.

But the darkness within him was relentless. There were days when Adam couldn't find the strength to get out of bed, when the weight of his grief was too much to bear. He felt lost and alone, trapped in a cycle of pain and despair.

Yet, through it all, he sensed Dennis's presence, a comforting hand on his shoulder, a whisper in the wind. It was as if Dennis was guiding him, helping him find his way through the darkness. Adam clung to this feeling, using it as a lifeline, a beacon of hope in the midst of his sorrow.

Slowly, very slowly, Adam began to find small moments of peace. He would sit by the piano, his fingers tracing the keys, feeling a connection to Dennis. He started to write again, his words a reflection of his grief and his love. It was a painful process, but it was also a way to heal, to find a path forward.

He knew he would never stop loving Dennis, that the pain of his loss would always be a part of him. But he also knew that Dennis would want him to live, to find happiness again. It was a long and difficult journey, but with Dennis's spirit by his side, Adam began to find the strength to move forward.

6

A TOUCH FROM BEYOND

Adam's journey through grief was a slow and painful process, but the presence of Dennis's spirit provided a constant source of comfort and strength. There were moments when he could almost feel Dennis's touch, a gentle caress on his cheek, a reassuring hand on his shoulder. These touches from beyond were a reminder that Dennis was still with him, watching over him, guiding him through the darkness.

One evening, as Adam sat at the piano, he felt an overwhelming urge to play. It had been months since he had last touched the keys, but the feeling was too strong to ignore. With trembling fingers, he began to play one of Dennis's favorite pieces, the notes filling the room with a haunting beauty.

As he played, he felt a warmth envelop him, a sense of peace that he hadn't felt in a long time. It was as if Dennis was there, his spirit infusing the music with his love and passion. Adam closed his eyes, letting the music wash over him, feeling a connection to Dennis that transcended the physical world.

When he finished playing, he opened his eyes to find tears streaming down his face. But these were not tears of sorrow; they were tears of healing, of a love that had not been extinguished by death. In that moment, Adam knew that Dennis's spirit was still with him, a guiding light in his darkest hours.

Inspired by this experience, Adam began to

incorporate music into his daily routine. He would play the piano each morning, starting his day with a connection to Dennis. The music became a form of therapy, a way to express his emotions and find solace in the midst of his grief.

He also started writing again, pouring his feelings into his stories. The words flowed more easily now, each sentence a reflection of his journey through love and loss. His characters came to life, their struggles and triumphs mirroring his own. Writing became a way to honor Dennis's memory, to keep his spirit alive through the stories they had shared.

Friends and family noticed the change in Adam. He was still grieving, but there was a sense of hope in his eyes, a determination to move forward. They offered their support, encouraging him to pursue his passions and find joy in the things he loved.

Adam also began to reach out to others who had experienced loss. He joined a support group, sharing his story and listening to the stories of others. The connections he made were a source of comfort, a reminder that he was not alone in his grief. Together, they found strength in their shared experiences, helping each other navigate the difficult path of healing.

Through it all, Dennis's spirit remained a constant presence. Adam would often feel a gentle touch on his shoulder, a whisper in the wind, a sense of warmth that filled his heart. These moments were a reminder that love transcends the physical world, that the bond they had shared was unbreakable.

Adam knew that he would always carry the pain of losing Dennis, that the grief would never fully go away. But he also knew that Dennis would want him to live, to find happiness and joy in the world. With Dennis's spirit by his side, he began to embrace life again, finding beauty and meaning in the everyday moments.

As the months passed, Adam continued to play the piano and write, each day a step forward in his healing journey. He felt a sense of peace, knowing that Dennis's love was still with him, guiding him through the challenges and triumphs of life. The touch from beyond was a reminder that their love was eternal, a bond that could never be broken.

7

HAUNTING MEMORIES

Adam's journey of healing was not without its challenges. Despite the comforting presence of Dennis's spirit, the memories of their time together often haunted him, a bittersweet reminder of the love he had lost.

The first time he returned to the concert hall where Dennis had performed, Adam was overwhelmed with emotion. The stage, once filled with Dennis's vibrant presence, now felt empty and cold. As he stood there, memories flooded his mind – the way Dennis's fingers danced over the keys, the passionate intensity of his performances, the joy in his eyes as he played.

Adam closed his eyes, letting the memories wash over him. He could almost hear the music, feel the energy of the crowd, see Dennis's smile. The pain of his loss was sharp, but there was also a sense of gratitude for the time they had shared. He knew that Dennis's spirit was with him, a comforting presence in the midst of his sorrow.

He began to visit other places that held special memories. The coffee shop where they had their first date, the park where they would walk hand in hand, the restaurant where Dennis had proposed. Each place brought a wave of emotions, a mix of joy and sadness, love and loss.

One day, while visiting their favorite park, Adam sat on a bench and closed his eyes. He could feel the warmth of the sun on his face, the gentle breeze rustling the leaves, the distant sound of laughter. It was a peaceful moment, a reminder of the simple joys they had shared.

As he sat there, he felt a gentle touch on his shoulder, a familiar warmth that filled his heart. He knew that Dennis was with him, a silent guardian watching over him. The presence was a source of comfort, a reminder that their love transcended the physical world.

Adam began to find solace in these memories, allowing himself to feel the emotions they brought. He realized that the pain of his loss was a reflection of the deep love they had shared, a testament to the bond that had not been broken by death. The memories, though haunting, were also a source of strength and healing.

He started to write about his experiences, turning his grief into stories that resonated with others. His characters were reflections of his journey, their struggles and triumphs a mirror of his own. Writing became a way to process his emotions, to honor Dennis's memory, to keep his spirit alive.

Through his writing, Adam found a sense of purpose. He wanted to share his story, to let others know that love endures, that healing is possible even in the midst of profound loss. His words touched the hearts of many, offering a beacon of hope to those who were struggling with their own grief.

As he continued to write, Adam felt Dennis's presence more strongly. There were moments when he could almost hear Dennis's voice, offering words of encouragement and love. These moments were a source of comfort, a reminder that Dennis was still with him, guiding him through the darkness.

The memories, though haunting, became a source of strength. They were a testament to the love that had not been extinguished by death, a reminder that Dennis's spirit was still with him. Adam found peace in the knowledge that their love was eternal, a bond that could never be broken.

8

SILENT GUARDIAN

Dennis's spirit continued to watch over Adam, a silent guardian guiding him through the challenges of life. There were moments when Adam could feel Dennis's presence more strongly, a comforting touch that filled his heart with warmth and love.

One evening, as Adam was working on his latest manuscript, he felt a sudden surge of inspiration. The words flowed effortlessly, each sentence a reflection of his journey through love and loss. He felt Dennis's presence, a guiding hand that helped him find the right words, the perfect expressions of his emotions.

As he wrote, Adam felt a sense of peace, a connection to Dennis that transcended the physical world. The pain of his loss was still there, but it was tempered by the love that had not been extinguished by death. Dennis's spirit was a constant presence, a source of strength and comfort.

Adam also began to notice small signs that Dennis was with him. A favorite song would play on the radio at just the right moment, a breeze would rustle the curtains as if someone had brushed past them, a faint scent of Dennis's cologne would linger in the air. These signs were a reminder that Dennis's spirit was still with him, watching over him, guiding him.

One day, while walking through the park, Adam felt a sudden urge to sit by the lake. It was a place they had often visited together, a spot where they would sit and talk for hours, sharing their dreams and hopes. As he sat there, he felt a sense of peace, a connection to Dennis that filled his heart with love.

He closed his eyes, letting the memories wash over him. He could almost hear Dennis's laughter, feel his touch, see his smile. The pain of his loss was still there, but it was accompanied by a deep sense of gratitude for the time they had shared, for the love that had not been diminished by death.

In that moment, Adam felt a gentle touch on his shoulder, a familiar warmth that filled his heart. He knew that Dennis was with him, a silent guardian watching over him. The presence was a source of comfort, a reminder that their love transcended the physical world.

As the months passed, Adam began to embrace life again. He found joy in the simple moments, in the beauty of the world around him, in the love and support of his friends and family. Dennis's spirit was a constant presence, a guiding light that helped him navigate the challenges and triumphs of life.

Adam also found love again. It was a gradual process, a journey of healing and self-discovery. He met someone who understood his pain, who accepted him for who he was, who loved him with a depth and intensity that mirrored his own. It was a different kind of love, but it was no less profound.

Dennis's spirit remained a constant presence, a silent guardian watching over him. Adam knew that Dennis would always be a part of him, that their love was eternal. He felt a sense of peace, knowing that Dennis was happy for him, that he wanted him to find joy and happiness in life.

As he continued to write, Adam felt a renewed sense of purpose. He wanted to share his story, to let others know that love endures, that healing is possible even in the midst of profound loss. His words touched the hearts of many, offering a beacon of hope to those who were struggling with their own grief.

Through it all, Dennis's spirit remained a constant presence, a source of strength and comfort. Adam found peace in the knowledge that their love was eternal, a bond that could never be broken. The silent guardian was always with him, guiding him through the darkness, helping him find the light.

9

THE ECHO OF LAUGHTER

As Adam continued his journey of healing, he found solace in the memories of Dennis's laughter. It was a sound that had brought so much joy and light into his life, a reminder of the happy moments they had shared. The echo of Dennis's laughter became a source of comfort, a beacon of hope that guided him through the darkest days.

Adam often found himself reminiscing about the times they had spent together, the simple moments that had brought them so much happiness. He remembered the way Dennis would laugh at his jokes, the sound of his laughter filling the room with warmth and love. It was a memory that brought both tears and smiles, a reminder of the love that had not been diminished by death.

One evening, as Adam sat at the piano, he felt a sudden urge to play one of Dennis's favorite pieces. The notes flowed effortlessly, each chord a reflection of the love they had shared. As he played, he felt a sense of peace, a connection to Dennis that transcended the physical world.

When he finished playing, he closed his eyes and let the memories wash over him. He could almost hear Dennis's laughter, feel his touch, see his smile. The pain of his loss was still there, but it was accompanied by a deep sense of gratitude for the time they had shared, for the love that had not been extinguished by death.

Adam began to incorporate these moments of

reminiscence into his daily routine. Each morning, he would sit by the piano and play one of Dennis's favorite pieces, letting the music fill the room with the echoes of their love. It was a ritual that brought him comfort, a way to keep Dennis's spirit alive in his heart.

He also started to write about these memories, turning his grief into stories that resonated with others. His characters were reflections of his journey, their struggles and triumphs a mirror of his own. Writing became a way to process his emotions, to honor Dennis's memory, to keep his spirit alive.

Through his writing, Adam found a sense of purpose. He wanted to share his story, to let others know that love endures, that healing is possible even in the midst of profound loss. His words touched the hearts of many, offering a beacon of hope to those who were struggling with their own grief.

Adam also began to reach out to others who had

experienced loss. He joined a support group, sharing his story and listening to the stories of others. The connections he made were a source of comfort, a reminder that he was not alone in his grief. Together, they found strength in their shared experiences, helping each other navigate the difficult path of healing.

Through it all, Dennis's spirit remained a constant presence. Adam would often feel a gentle touch on his shoulder, a whisper in the wind, a sense of warmth that filled his heart. These moments were a reminder that Dennis was still with him, watching over him, guiding him through the darkness.

As the months passed, Adam continued to embrace life again. He found joy in the simple moments, in the beauty of the world around him, in the love and support of his friends and family. Dennis's spirit was a constant presence, a guiding light that helped him navigate the challenges and triumphs of life.

Adam also found love again. It was a gradual process, a journey of healing and self-discovery. He met someone who understood his pain, who accepted him for who he was, who loved him with a depth and intensity that mirrored his own. It was a different kind of love, but it was no less profound.

Dennis's spirit remained a constant presence, a silent guardian watching over him. Adam knew that Dennis would always be a part of him, that their love was eternal. He felt a sense of peace, knowing that Dennis was happy for him, that he wanted him to find joy and happiness in life.

As he continued to write, Adam felt a renewed sense of purpose. He wanted to share his story, to let others know that love endures, that healing is possible even in the midst of profound loss. His words touched the hearts of many, offering a beacon of hope to those who were struggling with their own grief.

Through it all, Dennis's spirit remained a constant presence, a source of strength and comfort. Adam found peace in the knowledge that their love was eternal, a bond that could never be broken. The echo of Dennis's laughter was always with him, a reminder of the love that had brought so much joy and light into his life.

10

FINDING STRENGTH

Adam's journey of healing was a testament to the resilience of the human spirit. Despite the overwhelming grief and the constant reminders of his loss, he found strength in the love he had shared with Dennis and the comforting presence of Dennis's spirit.

One day, while visiting the park, Adam decided to take a walk along the path they had often traveled together. The familiar sights and sounds brought a wave of emotions, but there was also a sense of peace. He could almost feel Dennis walking beside him, their hands intertwined, their laughter echoing through the trees.

As he walked, Adam reflected on the strength he had found in the midst of his grief. He realized that Dennis had given him a gift, a love that was so profound and enduring that it had the power to transcend death. This realization filled him with a renewed sense of purpose, a determination to live his life in a way that honored Dennis's memory.

Adam began to embrace new opportunities and challenges. He took on new writing projects, exploring different genres and styles. His work was infused with the depth of emotion he had experienced, resonating with readers in a way that was both powerful and profound. He found joy in the creative process, a sense of fulfillment that had been missing since Dennis's death.

He also started to engage more with his friends

and family, accepting their support and offering his own in return. The connections he made were a source of comfort, a reminder that he was not alone in his journey. Together, they shared their experiences, their joys and sorrows, finding strength in their shared humanity.

One evening, as Adam sat by the piano, he felt a surge of inspiration. He began to compose a piece of music, a tribute to Dennis and the love they had shared. The notes flowed effortlessly, each chord a reflection of his journey through grief and healing. When he finished, he felt a sense of peace, a connection to Dennis that transcended the physical world.

The composition became a part of his daily routine. Each morning, he would play the piece, letting the music fill the room with the echoes of their love. It was a ritual that brought him comfort, a way to keep Dennis's spirit alive in his heart.

Adam also found joy in new experiences. He traveled to new places, explored new hobbies, and met new people. Each experience was a step forward in his healing journey, a reminder that life was filled with beauty and meaning. He embraced these moments, finding strength in the knowledge that Dennis's spirit was with him, guiding him through the challenges and triumphs of life.

As he continued to write and compose, Adam felt a renewed sense of purpose. He wanted to share his story, to let others know that love endures, that healing is possible even in the midst of profound loss. His words and music touched the hearts of many, offering a beacon of hope to those who were struggling with their own grief.

Through it all, Dennis's spirit remained a constant presence. Adam would often feel a gentle touch on his shoulder, a whisper in the wind, a sense of warmth that filled his heart. These moments were a reminder that Dennis was still with him, watching over him, guiding him through the darkness.

Adam found peace in the knowledge that their love was eternal, a bond that could never be broken. The strength he had found in the midst of his grief was a testament to the power of love, a reminder that even in the darkest moments, there is always a glimmer of hope.

As he continued his journey, Adam embraced life with a renewed sense of purpose and joy. He found beauty in the everyday moments, in the love and support of his friends and family, in the creative process that had become his refuge. Through it all, Dennis's spirit remained a constant presence, a guiding light that helped him find the strength to move forward.

11

THE FIRST SMILE

The first genuine smile that graced Adam's lips after Dennis's death was a moment of profound significance. It happened one afternoon while he was sitting in a quaint little café, working on his latest manuscript. The place was bustling with life, the sound of laughter and conversation creating a warm, inviting atmosphere.

As Adam sipped his coffee and typed away, he noticed a young couple at a nearby table. They were laughing, sharing stories and stolen glances, their happiness palpable. For a moment, Adam felt a pang of sadness, a reminder of the joy he had lost. But then, something unexpected happened. He felt a warmth spread through his chest, a gentle reminder of the love he had shared with Dennis.

Adam watched the couple, their joy infectious. He remembered the countless times he and Dennis had sat in similar cafés, lost in their own world of love and laughter. The memory brought a smile to his lips, a genuine expression of happiness that he hadn't felt in a long time. It was a moment of healing, a reminder that love's memory could bring joy even in the midst of grief.

As he left the café, Adam felt lighter, as if a weight had been lifted from his shoulders. The smile on his face was a testament to the progress he had made, a sign that he was beginning to find his way through the darkness. He knew that the journey was far from over, but this small moment of happiness was a beacon of hope, a reminder that life still held beauty and joy.

Inspired by this experience, Adam began to seek out more moments of joy. He reconnected with old friends, joined new social groups, and embraced

new hobbies. He found solace in the laughter and companionship of others, discovering that he could experience happiness without diminishing the love he still held for Dennis.

One day, while walking through the park, Adam came across a group of children playing a lively game of soccer. Their laughter and enthusiasm were infectious, and he found himself drawn to their energy. He sat on a nearby bench, watching them with a smile on his face, his heart lightened by their innocence and joy.

As he sat there, a man around his age approached and sat beside him. "Beautiful day, isn't it?" the man said, his voice friendly and warm.

Adam turned to him and nodded. "It really is. The kids seem to be having a lot of fun."

The man extended his hand. "I'm James, by the way. My nephew is one of the kids playing. He's the one in the red shirt."

Adam shook his hand. "I'm Adam. Nice to meet you, James."

They struck up a conversation, talking about the park, the kids, and eventually sharing bits of their own lives. Adam felt an unexpected connection with James, a sense of ease and understanding that was both comforting and intriguing. As the sun began to set, they exchanged phone numbers, promising to meet again.

Over the following weeks, Adam and James grew closer. They spent time together, exploring the city, trying new restaurants, and sharing their passions. James was an artist, and his creativity and zest for life were refreshing for Adam. Their friendship blossomed naturally, and Adam found himself looking forward to their time together.

As their bond deepened, Adam felt conflicted. He was still grieving for Dennis, and the idea of moving on felt like a betrayal. But Dennis's presence, the silent guardian who watched over him, seemed to encourage him to embrace this new connection. He felt Dennis's approval in the gentle touches, the whispers in the wind, the moments of warmth that filled his heart.

One evening, after a particularly enjoyable day spent exploring an art exhibit, James invited Adam to his apartment for dinner. They cooked together, laughing and sharing stories, the atmosphere filled with a sense of ease and companionship. After dinner, they sat on the couch, a comfortable silence enveloping them.

James turned to Adam; his expression serious yet tender. "Adam, I know you've been through a lot, and I don't want to push you into anything you're not ready for. But I care about you, and I want you to know that I'm here for you, whatever you need."

Adam felt a rush of emotions, gratitude, fear, and a glimmer of hope. He looked into James's eyes, seeing the sincerity and affection there. "Thank you, James. That means a lot to me. I've been struggling with moving forward, but I feel like Dennis would want me to find happiness again."

James reached out and took Adam's hand, a gentle yet firm grip. "I believe that too. And whatever happens, just know that I'm here for you."

In that moment, Adam felt a sense of peace, a reassurance that he was not betraying Dennis by finding happiness again. He felt Dennis's presence, a silent affirmation of his new journey. The first smile that had graced his lips in the café was just the beginning, a sign that he was on the path to healing and love.

12

SHADOWS OF THE PAST

Despite the growing bond between Adam and James, the shadows of the past still lingered. Adam often found himself haunted by memories of Dennis, moments of profound love and deep sorrow that surfaced unexpectedly. These memories, though bittersweet, were a testament to the love that had shaped his life.

One evening, as Adam was going through a box of Dennis's belongings, he came across an old photo album. The pictures captured the essence of their relationship, each image a snapshot of their love and happiness. Adam's heart ached as he flipped through the pages, tears streaming down his face as he relived the moments they had shared.

James found Adam sitting on the floor, surrounded by photographs, his face wet with tears. He approached quietly, sitting beside him and placing a comforting hand on his shoulder. "It's okay to feel this way, Adam. Those memories are a part of who you are, and they always will be."

Adam looked at James, his eyes filled with a mixture of grief and gratitude. "I miss him so much, James. Sometimes it feels like the pain will never go away."

James pulled him into a gentle embrace. "I know, and I'm here for you. You don't have to go through this alone."

Their relationship was a delicate balance, a dance between the past and the present. Adam was grateful for James's understanding and patience, his willingness to support him through his grief. It was a journey they navigated together; each step forward accompanied by the silent presence of Dennis's spirit.

Adam continued to write; his work infused with the depth of his emotions. He poured his heart into his stories, crafting narratives that reflected his own journey of love, loss, and healing. His characters grappled with their own shadows, finding strength in their connections and the enduring power of love.

One day, Adam received an invitation to speak at a local writer's conference. The opportunity was both exciting and daunting, a chance to share his story and his work with a broader audience. He felt a surge of anxiety, but also a sense of purpose. Dennis had always encouraged him to pursue his dreams, and this was a way to honor that encouragement.

James accompanied him to the conference, offering his unwavering support. As Adam stood before the audience, he felt a mixture of nerves and anticipation. He began to speak, sharing his journey through grief and the healing power of love. His words resonated with the audience, many of whom had their own stories of loss and resilience.

After the presentation, Adam was approached by numerous attendees, each one expressing their gratitude and sharing their own experiences. The connections he made were a source of comfort, a reminder that he was not alone in his journey. He felt a renewed sense of purpose, a determination to use his writing to offer hope and healing to others.

Through it all, Dennis's spirit remained a constant presence. Adam felt his touch in the moments of doubt, his warmth in the moments of joy, his guidance in the moments of uncertainty. The shadows of the past were a reminder of the love that had shaped his life, a testament to the bond that could never be broken.

As Adam continued to navigate his relationship with James, he found a delicate balance between honoring the past and embracing the future. James's understanding and patience were a source of strength, a reminder that it was possible to love again without diminishing the love he still held for Dennis.

Together, they faced the challenges and triumphs of life, each step forward a testament to their resilience and the enduring power of love. The shadows of the past were always there, but they were accompanied by the light of the present and the promise of the future.

13

THE HEALING TOUCH

Adam's journey of healing was marked by moments of profound connection and growth. The presence of Dennis's spirit, the support of James, and the strength he found within himself all contributed to his ongoing recovery. Each day brought new challenges and triumphs, each moment a step forward in his journey of love and loss.

One afternoon, while working on a new

manuscript, Adam felt a sudden urge to visit a nearby beach. It was a place that had held special significance for him and Dennis, a spot where they had shared countless sunsets and intimate conversations. The idea of returning there filled him with a mixture of apprehension and longing.

James, sensing his hesitation, offered to accompany him. "You don't have to do this alone, Adam. I'm here for you, whatever you need."

Adam nodded, grateful for James's support. Together, they made their way to the beach, the sound of the waves and the scent of the ocean bringing back a flood of memories. As they walked along the shore, Adam felt a sense of peace, a connection to Dennis that transcended the physical world.

They found a secluded spot and sat down, the sand warm beneath them, the sun casting a golden glow over the water. Adam closed his eyes, letting the memories wash over him. He could almost hear

Dennis's laughter, feel his touch, see his smile. The pain of his loss was still there, but it was accompanied by a deep sense of gratitude for the time they had shared.

James sat beside him, his presence a comforting anchor. "It's beautiful here, Adam. I can see why it meant so much to you and Dennis."

Adam nodded, tears filling his eyes. "We used to come here all the time. It was our special place, a sanctuary where we could be ourselves, away from the world."

James reached out and took Adam's hand, a gentle yet firm grip. "It's still a special place, Adam. And I'm honored to share it with you."

In that moment, Adam felt a profound sense of healing. The presence of Dennis's spirit, the love and support of James, and the beauty of the beach all came together, creating a space where he could embrace his grief and his joy. The healing touch of love was a powerful force, a reminder that he was not alone in his journey.

As the sun set, casting a brilliant array of colors over the water, Adam felt a sense of peace. He knew that Dennis was with him, watching over him, guiding him through the darkness. He also knew that James was a part of his journey, a source of strength and love that he was grateful for.

The healing touch of love continued to guide Adam in the days and weeks that followed. He found joy in the simple moments, in the beauty of the world around him, in the love and support of his friends and family. He embraced new experiences, finding fulfillment in his work, his hobbies, and his relationships.

Adam's writing flourished, his stories resonating with readers in a way that was both powerful and profound. He poured his heart into his work, crafting narratives that reflected his journey of love and loss. His characters grappled with their own struggles, finding strength in their connections and the enduring power of love.

Through it all, Dennis's spirit remained a constant presence. Adam felt his touch in the moments of doubt, his warmth in the moments of joy, his guidance in the moments of uncertainty. The healing touch of love was a reminder that their bond was eternal, a connection that could never be broken.

As Adam continued to navigate his relationship with James, he found a delicate balance between honoring the past and embracing the future. James's understanding and patience were a source of strength, a reminder that it was possible to love again without diminishing the love he still held for Dennis.

Together, they faced the challenges and triumphs of life, each step forward a testament to their resilience and the enduring power of love. The healing touch of love was always with them, guiding them through the darkness, helping them find the light.

14

A NEW LOVE

Adam's relationship with James blossomed into a deep and profound love. It was a different kind of love than what he had shared with Dennis, but it was no less significant. James brought a sense of joy and stability into Adam's life, a reminder that it was possible to find happiness and love again after profound loss.

Their bond grew stronger with each passing day, built on a foundation of understanding, patience, and mutual respect. James understood Adam's grief and supported him through his moments of sorrow, while Adam found solace in James's unwavering love and companionship.

One evening, as they sat together on the couch, James turned to Adam with a serious yet tender expression. "Adam, there's something I want to talk to you about."

Adam looked into James's eyes, sensing the importance of the moment. "What is it, James?"

James took a deep breath, his hand reaching out to hold Adam's. "I love you, Adam. I know that your heart will always hold a special place for Dennis, and I don't want to take that away. But I also want to build a future with you, to create new memories and share our lives together."

Tears filled Adam's eyes as he listened to James's words. "I love you too, James. You've been my rock, my support through everything. I want to build a future with you as well."

James smiled, his eyes filled with love and hope. "Then let's take this journey together, Adam. Let's embrace the love we have and create something beautiful."

Their decision to build a future together was a turning point in Adam's healing journey. It was a step forward, a testament to the strength of their love and their commitment to each other. They began to make plans, dreaming of a life filled with joy, adventure, and love.

Adam continued to write, his work reflecting the depth of his emotions and his journey of healing. His stories resonated with readers, offering a beacon of hope and a reminder that love endures, even in the face of profound loss. He found fulfillment in his work, a sense of purpose that brought him joy and satisfaction.

James, too, pursued his passions, his art reflecting the beauty and complexity of their love. Together, they supported each other's dreams, finding strength in their shared journey. Their love was a source of inspiration, a reminder that it was possible to find happiness and fulfillment after loss.

One day, while walking through the park, Adam felt a familiar warmth envelop him. It was Dennis's presence, a gentle reminder that he was still watching over him. Adam closed his eyes, feeling the love and support of both Dennis and James, a connection that transcended the physical world.

As he opened his eyes, Adam turned to James, his heart filled with gratitude and love. "Thank you for being there for me, James. For loving me and supporting me through everything."

James smiled; his eyes filled with tenderness. "I will always be here for you, Adam. Our love is strong, and together we can face anything."

Their journey was far from over, but Adam felt a sense of peace and fulfillment. He knew that

Dennis would always be a part of him, a guiding presence that had shaped his life. But he also knew that his love for James was just as significant, a testament to the resilience of the human heart and the enduring power of love.

Together, they embraced the future, their love a beacon of hope and joy. They found strength in their connection, their bond a reminder that it was possible to find happiness and fulfillment after loss. The love they shared was a beautiful testament to the power of love, a reminder that even in the darkest moments, there is always a glimmer of hope.

15

GUILT AND LONGING

As Adam continued to build his life with James, he sometimes felt a pang of guilt and longing for Dennis. These feelings were a natural part of his journey, a reflection of the deep love and connection he had shared with Dennis. But they were also a reminder of the resilience of the human heart and its capacity to love again.

One evening, as they sat together by the fire, Adam opened up to James about his feelings.

"James, there are times when I still feel guilty for moving on. I love you, but I also miss Dennis. It's a conflict that I struggle with."

James listened patiently, his hand gently resting on Adam's. "I understand, Adam. Your love for Dennis is a part of who you are, and it's natural to feel that way. I'm here to support you, and I want you to know that your feelings are valid."

Adam felt a sense of relief, grateful for James's understanding and compassion. "Thank you, James. Your support means everything to me."

As the months passed, Adam continued to navigate his feelings of guilt and longing. He found solace in the presence of Dennis's spirit, a comforting reminder that their love was eternal. Dennis's touch, the whispers in the wind, and the moments of warmth were a constant source of strength and guidance.

Adam also found comfort in his relationship with

James. Their bond was built on trust, understanding, and mutual respect. James's patience and support helped Adam to embrace his feelings, to honor his love for Dennis while also building a future with James.

One day, while visiting the beach that had held special significance for him and Dennis, Adam felt a profound sense of peace. The sound of the waves, the scent of the ocean, and the warmth of the sun all came together, creating a space where he could embrace his grief and his joy.

As he sat there, he felt a gentle touch on his shoulder, a familiar warmth that filled his heart. It was Dennis's presence, a silent affirmation of his journey. Adam closed his eyes, letting the memories wash over him, feeling the love and support of both Dennis and James.

He knew that it was possible to honor the past while embracing the future. The guilt and longing were a natural part of his journey, a testament to the depth of his love. But they were also a reminder of the resilience of the human heart and its capacity to heal and love again.

As he opened his eyes, Adam turned to James, his heart filled with gratitude and love. "Thank you for being there for me, James. For understanding and supporting me through everything."

James smiled; his eyes filled with tenderness. "I will always be here for you, Adam. Our love is strong, and together we can face anything."

Their journey was far from over, but Adam felt a sense of peace and fulfillment. He knew that Dennis would always be a part of him, a guiding presence that had shaped his life. But he also knew that his love for James was just as significant, a testament to the resilience of the human heart and the enduring power of love.

Together, they embraced the future, their love a beacon of hope and joy. They found strength in their connection, their bond a reminder that it was possible to find happiness and fulfillment after loss. The love they shared was a beautiful testament to the power of love, a reminder that even in the darkest moments, there is always a glimmer of hope.

16

SIGNS OF APPROVAL

Adam's relationship with James continued to flourish, and the presence of Dennis's spirit remained a comforting and guiding force. There were moments when Adam would feel a sudden warmth or hear a familiar melody, subtle signs that Dennis was still with him, watching over him and offering his silent approval.

One evening, as Adam and James were preparing dinner together, Adam felt a sudden urge to play one of Dennis's favorite pieces on the piano. He excused himself and walked over to the piano, his fingers dancing over the keys as the familiar melody filled the room. James listened, a smile on his face, appreciating the beauty of the music and the depth of emotion it conveyed.

When Adam finished playing, he turned to James with a wistful smile. "That was one of Dennis's favorites. I felt like playing it tonight for some reason."

James walked over and placed a hand on Adam's shoulder. "It was beautiful, Adam. I think Dennis would have loved it."

Adam nodded, feeling a sense of peace. "I think so too. It's moments like these that remind me that he's still with us, in spirit."

James smiled, his eyes filled with understanding and love. "I believe that too, Adam. And I think he's happy for us, happy that we've found love and happiness together."

The signs of Dennis's approval continued to manifest in various ways. There were times when Adam would be writing, and a sudden inspiration would strike him, as if guided by an unseen hand. He would often feel a gentle touch on his shoulder or hear a whisper in the wind, subtle reminders that Dennis was still a part of his life.

One day, while visiting a local art gallery with James, Adam felt a sudden warmth envelop him. They were standing in front of a painting that depicted a beautiful sunset over the ocean, a scene that reminded Adam of the many sunsets he had shared with Dennis. The feeling was so strong that Adam couldn't help but smile.

James noticed the change in Adam's expression and turned to him. "What is it, Adam?"

Adam shook his head, still smiling. "It's just... I felt a warmth, like Dennis was here with us. It's as if he's giving us his blessing."

James took Adam's hand, squeezing it gently. "I believe he is, Adam. And I think he's happy that we've found each other."

Their love continued to grow, strengthened by the signs of Dennis's approval and the deep bond they shared. Adam found joy in the simple moments, in the beauty of the world around him, in the love and support of James. He embraced new experiences, finding fulfillment in his work, his hobbies, and his relationships.

Adam's writing flourished, his stories resonating with readers in a way that was both powerful and profound. He poured his heart into his work, crafting narratives that reflected his journey of love and loss. His characters grappled with their own struggles, finding strength in their connections and the enduring power of love.

Through it all, Dennis's spirit remained a constant presence. Adam felt his touch in the moments of doubt, his warmth in the moments of joy, his guidance in the moments of uncertainty. The signs of Dennis's approval were a reminder that their bond was eternal, a connection that could never be broken.

As Adam continued to navigate his relationship with James, he found a delicate balance between honoring the past and embracing the future. James's understanding and patience were a source of strength, a reminder that it was possible to love again without diminishing the love he still held for Dennis.

Together, they faced the challenges and triumphs of life, each step forward a testament to their resilience and the enduring power of love. The signs of Dennis's approval were always with them, guiding them through the darkness, helping them find the light.

17

THE HEART'S DILEMMA

Adam's journey of healing was a complex and emotional one, marked by moments of joy, sorrow, and profound introspection. The love he had shared with Dennis and the new love he had found with James created a delicate balance, a heart's dilemma that he navigated with grace and courage.

One evening, as Adam was writing in his journal, he found himself reflecting on the complexities of his emotions. He loved James deeply, but there were times when the memories of Dennis would resurface, bringing a wave of longing and sorrow. It was a conflict that he struggled with, a reminder of the depth of his love and the enduring impact of his loss.

Adam decided to share his thoughts with James, knowing that open communication was essential to their relationship. "James, there's something I need to talk to you about. It's been on my mind for a while."

James looked at him with concern and understanding. "Of course, Adam. What's on your mind?"

Adam took a deep breath, gathering his thoughts. "I love you, James, more than words can express. But there are times when I still feel a deep longing for Dennis. It's a conflict that I struggle with, and I don't want it to affect our relationship."

James reached out and took Adam's hand, his touch gentle and reassuring. "Adam, I understand. Your love for Dennis is a part of who you are, and it's natural to feel that way. I don't see it as a conflict; I see it as a testament to the depth of your heart. You have room for both Dennis and me, and I respect and honor that."

Adam felt a surge of gratitude and relief. "Thank you, James. Your understanding means everything to me. I want to honor my love for Dennis while also building a future with you."

James smiled, his eyes filled with love and compassion. "We'll navigate this together, Adam. Our love is strong, and we can face anything that comes our way."

Their conversation brought a sense of clarity and peace to Adam. He realized that it was possible to honor his love for Dennis while also embracing his relationship with James. The heart's dilemma was a reflection of the depth of his emotions, a reminder that love's capacity was boundless and enduring.

Adam continued to write, his work reflecting the complexities of his journey. His stories resonated with readers, offering a glimpse into the human heart's ability to love deeply and navigate the challenges of loss and healing. His characters grappled with their own dilemmas, finding strength in their connections and the enduring power of love.

One day, while visiting a local bookstore with James, Adam felt a sudden surge of inspiration. He came across a book that captured his attention, a collection of poems that spoke to the themes of love, loss, and resilience. As he flipped through the pages, he felt a sense of connection to the words, a reflection of his own journey.

James noticed Adam's interest and smiled. "You should get it, Adam. It seems like it's speaking to you."

Adam nodded, feeling a sense of excitement and anticipation. "I think I will. It's like the author understands the complexities of love and loss, the same way I do."

The book became a source of inspiration for Adam, a reminder that he was not alone in his journey. He found solace in the words, a reflection of his own experiences and emotions. It was a testament to the power of storytelling, a reminder that the human heart's capacity for love and resilience was boundless.

As Adam continued to navigate his relationship with James, he found a delicate balance between honoring the past and embracing the future. James's understanding and patience were a source of strength, a reminder that it was possible to love again without diminishing the love he still held for Dennis.

Together, they faced the challenges and triumphs of life, each step forward a testament to their resilience and the enduring power of love. The heart's dilemma was a reflection of the depth of their emotions, a reminder that love's capacity was boundless and enduring.

18

UNSEEN PROTECTOR

Dennis's spirit remained a constant presence in Adam's life, an unseen protector who watched over him and guided him through his journey of healing and love. The subtle signs of Dennis's presence, the gentle touches, and the whispers in the wind were a source of comfort and strength, a reminder that their bond was eternal.

One afternoon, while Adam and James were hiking in the mountains, Adam felt a sudden urge to stop and take in the breathtaking view. The vast expanse of the landscape, the towering peaks, and the serene beauty of nature filled him with a sense of peace and connection.

As they stood there, Adam felt a gentle touch on his shoulder, a familiar warmth that filled his heart. He knew that Dennis was with them, an unseen protector who continued to watch over him. The feeling brought a sense of comfort and reassurance, a reminder that he was not alone in his journey.

James noticed the change in Adam's expression and turned to him. "What is it, Adam?"

Adam smiled, feeling the warmth of Dennis's presence. "I just felt Dennis's spirit with us. It's like he's giving us his blessing, watching over us as we navigate our journey together."

James took Adam's hand, his touch gentle and supportive. "I believe that too, Adam. And I'm grateful for the love and protection he continues to offer us."

Their hike continued, each step a testament to their bond and the unseen protector who guided them. The beauty of nature, the shared moments of joy, and the deep connection they felt were all reflections of the love that had brought them together.

Adam's writing continued to flourish, his stories resonating with readers in a way that was both powerful and profound. He poured his heart into his work, crafting narratives that reflected his journey of love and loss. His characters grappled with their own struggles, finding strength in their connections and the enduring power of love.

One day, while working on a new manuscript, Adam felt a sudden surge of inspiration. He began to write a story about an unseen protector, a spirit who watched over his loved ones and guided them through their challenges and triumphs. The story was a reflection of his own experiences, a testament to the enduring bond between him and Dennis.

As he wrote, Adam felt a sense of connection to Dennis, a reminder that their love was eternal. The words flowed effortlessly, each sentence a reflection of his journey and the strength he had found in the presence of his unseen protector.

The story became a source of inspiration for readers, offering a glimpse into the human heart's ability to love deeply and navigate the challenges of loss and healing. Adam received numerous letters from readers who had been touched by his words, each one a reminder of the impact of his work.

Through it all, Dennis's spirit remained a constant presence. Adam felt his touch in the moments of doubt, his warmth in the moments of joy, his guidance in the moments of uncertainty. The unseen protector was a reminder that their bond was eternal, a connection that could never be broken.

As Adam continued to navigate his relationship with James, he found a delicate balance between honoring the past and embracing the future. James's understanding and patience were a source of strength, a reminder that it was possible to love again without diminishing the love he still held for Dennis.

Together, they faced the challenges and triumphs of life, each step forward a testament to their resilience and the enduring power of love. The unseen protector was always with them, guiding them through the darkness, helping them find the light.

19

ACCEPTANCE AND GRIEF

Adam's journey of healing was a testament to the resilience of the human spirit and the enduring power of love. As he continued to navigate his relationship with James, he found a delicate balance between accepting his grief and embracing the love and happiness that life still had to offer.

One evening, as they sat together by the fire, Adam decided to share his thoughts with James.

"James, there's something I've been wanting to talk to you about. It's about accepting my grief and finding a way to honor both my love for Dennis and my love for you."

James looked at him with understanding and compassion. "Of course, Adam. I'm here to listen and support you in any way I can."

Adam took a deep breath, gathering his thoughts. "I realize that my grief for Dennis will always be a part of me, and that's okay. But I also know that it's possible to find joy and love again. You've shown me that, James. I want to honor my love for Dennis while also building a future with you."

James reached out and took Adam's hand, his touch gentle and reassuring. "I understand, Adam. Your love for Dennis is a part of who you are, and it's a part of what makes you so special. I want to support you in honoring that love while also embracing our future together."

Their conversation brought a sense of clarity and

peace to Adam. He realized that it was possible to accept his grief without letting it define him, to honor his love for Dennis while also building a future with James. The journey was not easy, but it was a path he was willing to take with courage and hope.

Adam continued to write, his work reflecting the complexities of his emotions and his journey of healing. His stories resonated with readers, offering a glimpse into the human heart's ability to love deeply and navigate the challenges of loss and healing. His characters grappled with their own dilemmas, finding strength in their connections and the enduring power of love.

One day, while visiting Dennis's grave, Adam felt a profound sense of peace. He knelt by the headstone, placing a bouquet of flowers and whispering a silent prayer. "Dennis, I will always love you. Your spirit is with me, guiding me through every step of my journey. Thank you for being my guardian, my protector, and my eternal love."

As he stood up, Adam felt a gentle breeze, a familiar touch that filled his heart with warmth. He knew that Dennis's spirit was with him, offering his silent approval and support. The feeling brought a sense of comfort and reassurance, a reminder that their bond was eternal.

Adam turned to James, who stood beside him, offering his unwavering support. "Thank you for being here with me, James. For understanding and supporting me through everything."

James smiled, his eyes filled with love and compassion. "I will always be here for you, Adam. Our love is strong, and together we can face anything."

Their journey was far from over, but Adam felt a sense of peace and fulfillment. He knew that Dennis would always be a part of him, a guiding presence that had shaped his life. But he also knew that his love for James was just as significant, a testament to the resilience of the human heart and the enduring power of love.

Together, they embraced the future, their love a beacon of hope and joy. They found strength in their connection, their bond a reminder that it was possible to find happiness and fulfillment after loss. The acceptance of his grief was a reminder that love's capacity was boundless and enduring.

20

THE LAST GOODBYE

Adam's journey of healing had brought him to a place of acceptance and peace. He had found a way to honor his love for Dennis while also building a future with James. The presence of Dennis's spirit remained a comforting and guiding force, a reminder that their bond was eternal.

One day, Adam felt a profound need to say a final goodbye to Dennis, a way to bring closure to his grief and fully embrace the future. He decided to visit the beach that had held special significance for them, a place where they had shared countless sunsets and intimate conversations.

James accompanied him, offering his unwavering support. As they walked along the shore, the sound of the waves and the scent of the ocean brought back a flood of memories. Adam felt a mixture of sorrow and gratitude, a reminder of the love that had shaped his life.

They found a secluded spot and sat down, the sand warm beneath them, the sun casting a golden glow over the water. Adam took a deep breath, feeling the weight of the moment. He closed his eyes, letting the memories wash over him, feeling the love and connection that had brought him to this place.

James sat beside him, his presence a comforting anchor. "Take your time, Adam. I'm here for you."

Adam nodded, feeling a sense of peace. He opened

his eyes and looked out at the horizon, the setting sun painting the sky with brilliant colors. "Dennis, I will always love you. You were my first true love, and you will always be a part of me. Thank you for the time we had together, for the love and joy you brought into my life."

He felt a gentle breeze, a familiar touch that filled his heart with warmth. Adam knew that Dennis was with him, offering his silent approval and support. The feeling brought a sense of comfort and reassurance, a reminder that their bond was eternal.

Adam turned to James, his eyes filled with love and gratitude. "Thank you for being here with me, James. For understanding and supporting me through everything."

James smiled; his eyes filled with tenderness. "I will always be here for you, Adam. Our love is strong, and together we can face anything."

The last goodbye was a moment of profound

significance for Adam. It was a way to bring closure to his grief, to honor his love for Dennis while also embracing his future with James. The journey was not easy, but it was a path he was willing to take with courage and hope.

Adam continued to write, his work reflecting the complexities of his emotions and his journey of healing. His stories resonated with readers, offering a glimpse into the human heart's ability to love deeply and navigate the challenges of loss and healing. His characters grappled with their own dilemmas, finding strength in their connections and the enduring power of love.

Through it all, Dennis's spirit remained a constant presence. Adam felt his touch in the moments of doubt, his warmth in the moments of joy, his guidance in the moments of uncertainty. The last goodbye was not an end, but a continuation of their eternal bond.

As Adam and James walked back along the shore,

hand in hand, they felt a sense of peace and fulfillment. They knew that their journey was far from over, but they were ready to face it together, their love a beacon of hope and joy.

Together, they embraced the future, their bond a reminder that it was possible to find happiness and fulfillment after loss. The last goodbye was a testament to the resilience of the human heart and the enduring power of love.

21

ETERNAL PROMISES

Adam and James's relationship continued to grow, built on a foundation of love, understanding, and mutual respect. The journey they had taken together had strengthened their bond, and they found joy and fulfillment in their shared experiences and dreams.

One evening, as they sat together by the fire, James turned to Adam with a serious yet tender expression. "Adam, there's something I want to talk to you about. It's about our future and the promises we make to each other."

Adam looked into James's eyes, sensing the importance of the moment. "What is it, James?"

James took a deep breath, gathering his thoughts. "I love you, Adam, more than words can express. We've been through so much together, and I want to continue building a life with you. I want us to make a promise to each other, a commitment to love and support one another through whatever comes our way."

Tears filled Adam's eyes as he listened to James's words. "I love you too, James. You've been my rock, my support through everything. I want to make that promise to you as well."

James reached out and took Adam's hand, his touch gentle and reassuring. "Let's promise to always be there for each other, to love and support one another through the highs and lows, to cherish the moments we have together."

Adam nodded, his heart filled with love and gratitude. "I promise, James. I will always be there for you, through everything. Our love is strong, and I believe we can face anything together."

Their commitment to each other brought a sense of peace and fulfillment to Adam. It was a promise that reflected the depth of their love and the resilience of their hearts. The journey they had taken together had been marked by challenges and triumphs, but their love had endured, growing stronger with each step forward.

Adam continued to write, his work reflecting the complexities of his emotions and his journey of healing. His stories resonated with readers, offering a glimpse into the human heart's ability to love deeply and navigate the challenges of loss and healing. His characters grappled with their own dilemmas, finding strength in their connections and the enduring power of love.

Through it all, Dennis's spirit remained a constant

presence. Adam felt his touch in the moments of doubt, his warmth in the moments of joy, his guidance in the moments of uncertainty. The eternal promises he had made to both Dennis and James were a reminder that love's capacity was boundless and enduring.

One day, while visiting a local park, Adam and James found a quiet spot by the lake. They sat together, the serene beauty of nature creating a space of peace and connection. Adam felt a gentle breeze, a familiar touch that filled his heart with warmth. He knew that Dennis's spirit was with them, offering his silent approval and support.

James turned to Adam, his eyes filled with love and tenderness. "This is a beautiful moment, Adam. I'm grateful for the love we share and the journey we've taken together."

Adam smiled, feeling a sense of peace. "Me too, James. Our love is strong, and I'm grateful for every moment we have together."

Their eternal promises were a testament to the resilience of the human heart and the enduring power of love. Together, they embraced the future, their bond a reminder that it was possible to find happiness and fulfillment after loss.

As they walked back along the path, hand in hand, they felt a sense of peace and fulfillment. They knew that their journey was far from over, but they were ready to face it together, their love a beacon of hope and joy.

Together, they embraced the future, their bond a reminder that it was possible to find happiness and fulfillment after loss. The eternal promises they had made to each other were a testament to the resilience of the human heart and the enduring power of love.

22

LOVE TRANSCENDS

Adam's journey of healing had taught him that love transcends the boundaries of time and space. The love he had shared with Dennis and the love he now shared with James were a testament to the boundless and enduring capacity of the human heart. Each day brought new experiences, challenges, and moments of joy, all of which were embraced with a sense of gratitude and love.

One afternoon, while Adam was working on his

latest manuscript, he felt a sudden surge of inspiration. The words flowed effortlessly, each sentence a reflection of his journey and the strength he had found in love. He realized that his stories were not just about loss and healing, but also about the transcendent power of love.

As he wrote, Adam felt a sense of connection to Dennis, a reminder that their bond was eternal. The presence of Dennis's spirit, the gentle touches, and the whispers in the wind were a constant source of comfort and guidance. He knew that Dennis's love would always be a part of him, shaping his life and his journey.

James entered the room, noticing the intensity of Adam's focus. "You look inspired, Adam. What's going on in that brilliant mind of yours?"

Adam looked up, a smile on his face. "I'm writing about the transcendent power of love, how it can overcome any obstacle and endure through time and space. It's a reflection of our journey and the love we share."

James walked over and placed a gentle kiss on Adam's forehead. "I love that, Adam. Your words have a way of touching the hearts of others and offering hope and inspiration."

Adam felt a surge of gratitude and love. "Thank you, James. Your support means everything to me."

Their relationship continued to flourish, built on a foundation of love, understanding, and mutual respect. They found joy in the simple moments, in the beauty of the world around them, in the love and support they shared. The transcendent power of love was a guiding force, a reminder that their bond was eternal and unbreakable.

One day, while visiting a local art gallery, Adam and James came across a painting that captured their attention. The artwork depicted a beautiful scene of a couple standing together, their hands intertwined, surrounded by a vibrant and colorful landscape. The painting was a reflection of their journey, a testament to the transcendent power of love.

Adam felt a deep connection to the painting, a sense of peace and fulfillment. "This reminds me of us, James. Our journey, our love, and the strength we've found together."

James nodded, his eyes filled with understanding and love. "It does, Adam. Our love is strong, and it transcends any obstacle we face."

Their love continued to inspire Adam's writing, his stories resonating with readers in a way that was both powerful and profound. He poured his heart into his work, crafting narratives that reflected his journey of love and loss. His characters grappled with their own struggles, finding strength in their connections and the enduring power of love.

Through it all, Dennis's spirit remained a constant

presence. Adam felt his touch in the moments of doubt, his warmth in the moments of joy, his guidance in the moments of uncertainty. The transcendent power of love was a reminder that their bond was eternal, a connection that could never be broken.

As Adam and James continued to navigate their relationship, they found a delicate balance between honoring the past and embracing the future. James's understanding and patience were a source of strength, a reminder that it was possible to love again without diminishing the love he still held for Dennis.

Together, they faced the challenges and triumphs of life, each step forward a testament to their resilience and the enduring power of love. The transcendent power of love was always with them, guiding them through the darkness, helping them find the light.

23

MOVING FORWARD

Adam's journey of healing had brought him to a place of acceptance and peace. He had found a way to honor his love for Dennis while also building a future with James. The presence of Dennis's spirit remained a comforting and guiding force, a reminder that their bond was eternal.

One evening, as they sat together by the fire, James turned to Adam with a serious yet tender expression. "Adam, there's something I want to talk to you about. It's about our future and the steps we want to take moving forward."

Adam looked into James's eyes, sensing the importance of the moment. "What is it, James?"

James took a deep breath, gathering his thoughts. "We've been through so much together, and I want to continue building a life with you. I think it's time we talk about taking the next step, about making our commitment to each other more formal."

Tears filled Adam's eyes as he listened to James's words. "I love you, James. You've been my rock, my support through everything. I want to take that step with you, to build a future together."

James reached out and took Adam's hand, his touch gentle and reassuring. "Let's make a commitment to each other, Adam. Let's move forward together and build a life filled with love and joy."

Their decision to take the next step in their relationship brought a sense of peace and fulfillment to Adam. It was a promise that reflected the depth of their love and the resilience of their hearts. The journey they had taken together had been marked by challenges and triumphs, but their love had endured, growing stronger with each step forward.

Adam continued to write, his work reflecting the complexities of his emotions and his journey of healing. His stories resonated with readers, offering a glimpse into the human heart's ability to love deeply and navigate the challenges of loss and healing. His characters grappled with their own dilemmas, finding strength in their connections and the enduring power of love.

One day, while visiting a local park, Adam and James found a quiet spot by the lake. They sat together, the serene beauty of nature creating a space of peace and connection. Adam felt a gentle breeze, a familiar touch that filled his heart with warmth. He knew that Dennis's spirit was with them, offering his silent approval and support.

James turned to Adam, his eyes filled with love and tenderness. "This is a beautiful moment, Adam. I'm grateful for the love we share and the journey we've taken together."

Adam smiled, feeling a sense of peace. "Me too, James. Our love is strong, and I'm grateful for every moment we have together."

Their commitment to each other was a testament to the resilience of the human heart and the enduring power of love. Together, they embraced the future, their bond a reminder that it was possible to find happiness and fulfillment after loss.

As they walked back along the path, hand in hand, they felt a sense of peace and fulfillment. They knew that their journey was far from over, but they were ready to face it together, their love a beacon of hope and joy.

Together, they embraced the future, their bond a reminder that it was possible to find happiness and fulfillment after loss. The commitment they had made to each other was a testament to the resilience of the human heart and the enduring power of love.

24

THE GIFT OF MEMORY

Adam's journey of healing had taught him that memories are a precious gift, a testament to the love and experiences that shape our lives. The memories he had of Dennis were a source of comfort and strength, a reminder of the love that had brought so much joy and meaning to his life. As he continued to build his future with James, he found a way to cherish these memories while also embracing the new experiences and moments of joy they shared.

One evening, as Adam and James were looking through old photo albums, Adam felt a mixture of emotions. The pictures captured the essence of his life with Dennis, each image a snapshot of their love and happiness. But there were also new memories, moments he had shared with James, that brought a sense of joy and fulfillment.

James noticed the change in Adam's expression and placed a comforting hand on his shoulder. "It's okay to feel this way, Adam. These memories are a part of who you are, and they always will be."

Adam nodded, feeling a sense of peace. "Thank you, James. The memories I have with Dennis are precious to me, and they always will be. But I'm also grateful for the new memories we're creating together."

James smiled, his eyes filled with love and understanding. "Our journey is just beginning,

Adam. Let's continue to create beautiful memories together."

The gift of memory became a source of inspiration for Adam's writing. He poured his heart into his work, crafting stories that reflected his journey of love and loss. His characters grappled with their own struggles, finding strength in their connections and the enduring power of love. His stories resonated with readers, offering a glimpse into the human heart's ability to love deeply and navigate the challenges of loss and healing.

One day, while visiting a local bookstore, Adam came across a journal that caught his attention. It was beautifully bound, with blank pages waiting to be filled with thoughts and memories. He decided to buy it, feeling a sense of excitement and anticipation.

As he began to write in the journal, Adam found a sense of peace and fulfillment. He documented his journey, the memories of his time with Dennis, and the new experiences he was sharing with James. The journal became a reflection of his life, a testament to the love that had shaped his past and the love that was guiding his future.

Adam also found joy in sharing these memories with others. He spoke at local events, offering words of hope and inspiration to those who were struggling with their own grief. His message was clear: love endures, and healing is possible even in the face of profound loss. The gift of memory was a reminder that the love we share with others is eternal, a connection that can never be broken.

Through it all, Dennis's spirit remained a constant presence. Adam felt his touch in the moments of doubt, his warmth in the moments of joy, his guidance in the moments of uncertainty. The gift of memory was a reminder that their bond was eternal, a connection that could never be broken.

As Adam and James continued to navigate their relationship, they found a delicate balance between honoring the past and embracing the future. James's understanding and patience were a source of strength, a reminder that it was possible to love again without diminishing the love he still held for Dennis.

Together, they faced the challenges and triumphs of life, each step forward a testament to their resilience and the enduring power of love. The gift of memory was always with them, guiding them through the darkness, helping them find the light.

25

FOREVER IN MY HEART

Adam's journey of healing had brought him to a place of acceptance, peace, and profound love. The memories of Dennis and the love he now shared with James were a testament to the boundless and enduring capacity of the human heart. Each day brought new experiences, challenges, and moments of joy, all of which were embraced with a sense of gratitude and love.

One evening, as Adam and James sat together by

the fire, Adam decided to share his thoughts with James. "James, there's something I want to talk to you about. It's about the journey we've taken together and the love that has brought us to this place."

James looked into Adam's eyes, sensing the importance of the moment. "What is it, Adam?"

Adam took a deep breath, gathering his thoughts. "I want you to know that you have brought so much joy and love into my life. The journey we've taken together has been filled with challenges and triumphs, and I am grateful for every moment. Dennis will always be a part of my heart, but so are you. I love you, James."

Tears filled James's eyes as he listened to Adam's words. "I love you too, Adam. You've shown me what it means to love deeply and to find strength in the face of loss. Our love is strong, and I am grateful for every moment we have together."

Their love continued to inspire Adam's writing,

his stories resonating with readers in a way that was both powerful and profound. He poured his heart into his work, crafting narratives that reflected his journey of love and loss. His characters grappled with their own struggles, finding strength in their connections and the enduring power of love.

One day, while visiting a local park, Adam and James found a quiet spot by the lake. They sat together, the serene beauty of nature creating a space of peace and connection. Adam felt a gentle breeze, a familiar touch that filled his heart with warmth. He knew that Dennis's spirit was with them, offering his silent approval and support.

James turned to Adam, his eyes filled with love and tenderness. "This is a beautiful moment, Adam. I'm grateful for the love we share and the journey we've taken together."

Adam smiled, feeling a sense of peace. "Me too, James. Our love is strong, and I'm grateful for every moment we have together."

The journey they had taken together had been marked by challenges and triumphs, but their love had endured, growing stronger with each step forward. The memories of Dennis and the love they now shared were a testament to the resilience of the human heart and the enduring power of love.

Adam's journey of healing had taught him that love transcends the boundaries of time and space. The love he had shared with Dennis and the love he now shared with James were a testament to the boundless and enduring capacity of the human heart. Each day brought new experiences, challenges, and moments of joy, all of which were embraced with a sense of gratitude and love.

Through it all, Dennis's spirit remained a constant presence. Adam felt his touch in the moments of doubt, his warmth in the moments of joy, his guidance in the moments of uncertainty. The memories of Dennis and the love he now shared with James were a reminder that their bond was eternal, a connection that could never be broken.

As Adam and James continued to navigate their relationship, they found a delicate balance between honoring the past and embracing the future. James's understanding and patience were a source of strength, a reminder that it was possible to love again without diminishing the love he still held for Dennis.

Together, they faced the challenges and triumphs of life, each step forward a testament to their resilience and the enduring power of love. The memories of Dennis and the love they now shared were a reminder that the human heart has an infinite capacity to love, to heal, and to find joy.

Forever in his heart, Adam carried the love and memories of Dennis. But he also embraced the love he now shared with James, a love that brought him joy, fulfillment, and a sense of purpose. The journey was far from over, but Adam was ready to face it with courage, hope, and an open heart.

Together, Adam and James embraced the future, their bond a reminder that it was possible to find happiness and fulfillment after loss. The love they shared was a beautiful testament to the power of love, a reminder that even in the darkest moments, there is always a glimmer of hope.

ABOUT THE AUTHOR

Aiden Blake, a proud gay man in his 30s, writes with a heart full of experience and a soul rich with empathy. Having walked the path of self-discovery and faced the challenges that come with living authentically, Aiden's journey is a testament to the power of love, resilience, and unwavering courage.

Aiden's writing is deeply personal and profoundly impactful, drawing from his own experiences to create stories that resonate with readers from all walks of life. He understands the beauty of diversity and the strength found in the LGBTQ+ community, and he channels this understanding into every word he writes.

In a world that can often be unkind, Aiden's work shines as a beacon of hope and affirmation. He believes that there is someone for everyone, and his stories are a celebration of love in all its forms.

Whether you are single or coupled, Aiden's writing reminds you that you are seen, valued, and deeply loved.

Aiden lives his life with authenticity and pride, finding inspiration in the everyday triumphs and challenges of the LGBTQ+ community. His dedication to storytelling is matched only by his commitment to being a voice for those who have ever felt different or alone.

Through his books, Aiden aims to create a space where everyone can see themselves reflected, where every love story is honored, and where every reader is reminded of their inherent worth. Join Aiden on a journey of love, resilience, and the unbreakable spirit of the human heart.

ACKNOWLEDGMENTS

To the LGBTQ+ Community—

This book is for you, and it is because of you. Your stories, your courage, and your love inspire me every day. I am deeply grateful for the support, solidarity, and sense of belonging I have found within this incredible community. Your resilience and authenticity have been a guiding light for me, and I hope my words can honor your experiences and reflect the strength we share.

To those who have shared their stories with me, thank you. Your openness and vulnerability have enriched my understanding and deepened my compassion. Your lives are a testament to the beauty of diversity and the power of living true to oneself.

To the couples who have shown the world that love knows no bounds, and to the individuals who have stood strong in their truth, thank you for your bravery. You remind us all that there is someone for everyone, and that love, in all its forms, is worth celebrating and fighting for.

To my friends and family, your unwavering support has been my anchor. Thank you for believing in me and standing by me through every challenge and triumph. Your love has been my greatest source of strength.

To every reader who has ever felt different, who has ever loved against the odds, who has ever faced the world with courage in their hearts—this book is for you. May you always remember that you are seen, valued, and deeply loved.

Lastly, to those who continue to fight for equality, acceptance, and love in all its forms, thank you. Your efforts pave the way for a brighter, more inclusive future for us all.